The Cat Burglars

By
Gary J. Spack

Illustrations by Kalpart

Strategic Book Publishing and Rights Co.

Strategic Book Publishing and Rights Co., LLC
USA | Singapore
www.sbpra.com

For information about special discounts for bulk purchases, please contact Strategic Book Publishing and Rights Co., LLC. Special Sales, at bookorder@sbpra.net.

ISBN: 978-1-948260-76-3

This book is dedicated to all my students, past and present, who inspire me every day and who wanted me to write a book where the main characters were animals. I also want to thank my wife Michele for all her undying love and support. I couldn't do it without you! Lastly, this is for all the pet lovers who think of their four-legged companions as members of the family.

"I can't believe you talked me into this, Phoebe. Look at the mess you've gotten us into."

"Well, Boomer, you must not have thought it was too bad, since you went along with it."

"How could I have been so gullible? We'll be cat burglars to stop a cat burglar? Really, Phoebe?"

Phoebe and Boomer are sister and brother, and they just happen to be cats. They live in a wonderful household with their humans, John and Catherine Michaels, and a German shepherd puppy named Gus. Though still considered a puppy, Gus was six months old and nearly fully grown.

One night, while everyone was comfortably sitting on their favorite piece of furniture in the family room, a news flash came across the television screen that there were cat burglars in the Michaels' neighborhood.

"Oh my goodness," said Mrs. Michaels. "What if they come to our house?"

"I don't think we have to worry," replied Mr. Michaels. "We don't really have anything that valuable and, after all, we have Gus. No cat burglar would dare come into our house with him around."

"Cat burglars?" Boomer said with a bewildered look on his face. "There are actually thieves who steal cats? What is wrong with this world? And what is going on with our humans? They don't seem to be concerned in the least bit, and the little concern they do show is not for us, but for some valuables. And they think Gus is going to protect us? He's the friendliest, cutest, and most trusting dog in the whole wide world! If anyone broke into our home, he'd lick them silly, and then probably take them on a guided tour of the house."

Before Boomer could continue with his rant, Phoebe cut him off.

"Boomer, the burglars aren't stealing cats. They steal jewelry and other valuables from peoples' houses. They are called 'cat burglars' because they are stealthy and sneaky, just like cats. But you are right about Mr. and Mrs. Michaels not being concerned and that Gus isn't going to stop any burglars."

"What do you think we should do then, Phoebe?"

"Actually, I have a brilliant idea. We'll protect them by becoming cat burglars."

"What!"

"Yes, cat burglars. We'll steal their things a little at a time so they won't notice they're gone, and then we'll hide them somewhere safe until the real cat burglars are caught."

"That's your brilliant idea?"

"Who better to be cat burglars than cats? Besides, I don't see you coming up with any solutions."

"Okay, I guess," said Boomer.

"Glad you see it my way. We'll start tonight."

When nighttime came and everyone was fast asleep, Phoebe and Boomer put their plan into action. With Phoebe leading the way, the two felines quietly made their way up the stairs, down the hallway, and into Mr. and Mrs. Michaels' bedroom.

"Come on, Boomer. The coast is clear. Everyone is sleeping, including Gus. Okay, now you jump up on the dresser, open the drawer, and take a bracelet. Then I'll jump up and take one. Got it?"

"Got it."

Boomer, not being quite as agile as Phoebe, jumped up on the dresser. He was bigger and heavier than she was too. He barely made it, and the dresser wobbled from his weight and near miss.

"Way to go," whispered Phoebe in an annoyed voice. "You almost crashed the dresser. I think you need to lay off the cat treats for a while."

"Oh, ha, ha, ha," retorted Boomer. "This isn't the time for insults, Phoebe."

11

"Fine. Now, watch how a real cat burglar does it."

Phoebe effortlessly launched herself upward with plenty of height and dropped as softly as a feather on the dresser right next to Boomer. Phoebe expertly grabbed a shiny bracelet with her mouth and jumped down as quietly and as gracefully as she had jumped up.

Unlike his sister, Boomer, after closing the dresser drawer, jumped down and landed with a thud. Phoebe cringed at the sound, certain that Boomer's thunderous, earthquake landing would wake the Michaels and Gus, plus half the neighbors on their street.

"Geez, Boomer. Did you have to send out seismic shockwaves when you landed?"

"Sorry."

"You've really got to cut back on the cat treats. You're going to get us caught. Let's go while they're still sound asleep."

"Okay, but where are we going to hide the jewelry?"

"I know the perfect place. We'll hide the stuff behind the chest of drawers in the dining room. There's enough space for us to get behind it, and the Michaels don't use the dining room much, so no one will see any of it. Let's go before someone wakes up."

Encouraged by the success of their first cat burglary, Phoebe and Boomer continued their nightly escapades without the Michaels or Gus knowing what they were doing. The real cat burglars were still stalking the neighborhood, and Phoebe and Boomer felt proud that they were protecting their humans' valuable belongings. Unfortunately, things were about to change.

It was Saturday evening, and Mr. and Mrs. Michaels were busy getting ready to go out for dinner. Phoebe, Boomer, and Gus were all settled on their favorite pieces of furniture, waiting to spend a lazy evening all by themselves. No sooner had they become comfortable than the peace and quiet was disturbed by a loud scream.

"Oh my gosh! John, come quick!"

"What is it?"

"The cat burglars were here! We've been robbed! Call the police!"

This, of course, caught the attention of not only Phoebe and Boomer, but Gus too.

"Did you hear that?" Gus asked. "The cat burglars broke into the house and stole the Michaels' jewelry. They must be really clever, because I didn't hear or see a thing."

No kidding, thought Boomer and Phoebe.

"I'm going to investigate and figure out what happened," declared Gus, and off he went.

"Looks like we're in big trouble now, Phoebe. Gus seems really determined to get to the bottom of this. What are we going to do?"

"Relax, Boomer. Sherlock Holmes there couldn't figure out where his own chew bone went if he carried it into another room himself."

"Well, what about the police? Mr. Michaels called them. They'll figure it out and then what? Kitty jail?"

"No one's going to kitty jail, so stop getting yourself all in a tizzy. I have another idea."

"Great! Another idea. Just what we need. Look how well your other idea worked out."

"Well, we did save the Michaels' jewelry, and now I'm going to save *us*."

"I can hardly wait to hear it."

"It's simple. Humans know that cats like to take things, because they either want attention or just want to play. We'll go on one more caper, but let them catch us in the act. They'll follow us and find our

18

hiding place. They'll see all their things and think we just wanted attention. They'll think it's adorable. They'll tell the police it was their cats and everyone will have a big laugh."

"Once again, it sounds pretty far out there, but it's the only thing we have, so we may as well try it."

In the meantime, the police arrived and were talking to Mr. and Mrs. Michaels and looking around. Gus was thrilled that the police were there and followed them everywhere they went.

"Okay, Boomer. If we're going to get caught, we may as well make a spectacle out of it and have the police catch us red-handed. Follow me."

Phoebe and Boomer nonchalantly walked past Mr. and Mrs. Michaels, the police, and Gus, and headed straight for their humans' bedroom. They went right to the dresser and, just as they had done almost every night for the past two weeks, jumped up onto the dresser, opened the top drawer, and each took a remaining piece of jewelry. They then proceeded to proudly march, one behind the other, with Phoebe leading the way, out of the bedroom, down the hallway, down

the stairs, and right past the police, Mr. and Mrs. Michaels, and Gus. Gus spotted the cat parade first and barked loudly, alerting everyone.

"Good boy," said one of the police officers, patting Gus on the head.

The police, the Michaels, and Gus all looked on in amazement as the cats walked right past them, as though not having a care in the world.

"Do you see that?" asked Mr. Michaels.

"I do, but I can't believe what I'm seeing," replied Mrs. Michaels.

"I'm assuming these are your cats?" asked the other officer.

"They are."

"Well, it looks like we might have solved the case," said the officer standing alongside Gus. "Let's follow them and see where they're taking these things."

Everyone followed and watched in astonishment as the two cats walked into the dining room and placed their loot behind the chest of drawers. The police officers pushed back the large piece of furniture. There, in a pile, was all the missing jewelry.

"Well, how about that," declared Mr. Michaels.

"I can't believe it," said Mrs. Michaels. "It was Phoebe and Boomer. I've heard of cats doing things like this, but I never knew *these* two did it. We must not be giving them enough attention. Poor babies. They're so cute and adorable."

All of a sudden, Gus was at attention—back straight, tail wagging furiously, and ears pointing straight up.

"What is it, boy?" queried Mr. Michaels.

No sooner had he asked that question than Gus sprang forward and went through the large doggie door to the outside. Everyone, including the police officers, followed. They heard loud barking, then growls, and then some pleading voices.

"Nice doggie! Good boy! Please don't bite us!"

Gus had two men, both dressed fully in black clothing, pinned up against the backyard wall. Each man had a satchel full of jewelry stolen from people throughout the neighborhood. Gus had actually caught the real cat burglars! The burglars had just robbed the neighbor's house and were making their escape over the wall with the intention of hitting the Michaels' house next.

"That's some dog you have there, Mr. and Mrs. Michaels," said one of the officers. "He'd make a fine police dog."

"He probably would," said Mrs. Michaels, "but we'd rather he just be our pet."

"Okay, folks. We'll take these two in for questioning and leave you to go about your evening. The case is closed, thanks to Gus."

"Thank you, officers," said Mr. and Mrs. Michaels.

Phoebe and Boomer were watching all of this from the big window in the kitchen.

"Can you believe Gus caught the burglars? *Gus?*" exclaimed Boomer.

"I know," said Phoebe. "Unbelievable. But, as they say, every dog has his day."

"And what about our day, Phoebe? We did save the Michaels' jewelry, even though they don't really know that."

"I think our day has arrived too. Didn't you hear Mrs. Michaels say how cute and adorable we are and how we need to get more attention?"

"Yes, and maybe more cat treats too?"

"I wouldn't be surprised, Boomer. Now, I'm going back to my chair. Our work here is done—until our next adventure."

"Phoebe!"

Review Requested:
If you loved this book, would you please provide a review at Amazon.com?

Thank You

CPSIA information can be obtained
at www.ICGtesting.com
Printed in the USA
LVHW070819011218
598886LV00014B/276/P